All the King's Tights

There are lots of Early Reader
stories you might enjoy.

Look at the back of the book or,
for a complete list, visit
www.orionchildrensbooks.co.uk

All the King's Tights

Maudie Smith

Illustrated by Ali Pye

Orion
Children's Books

ORION CHILDREN'S BOOKS

First published in Great Britain in 2016 by Hodder and Stoughton

1 3 5 7 9 10 8 6 4 2

Text copyright © Maudie Smith, 2016
Illustrations copyright © Ali Pye, 2016

The moral rights of the author and illustrator have been asserted.

A CIP catalogue record for this book
is available from the British Library.

ISBN 978 1 4440 1425 9

Printed and bound in China

The paper and board used in this book are from well-managed forests
and other responsible sources.

MIX
Paper from
responsible sources
FSC® C104740

Orion Children's Books
An imprint of
Hachette Children's Group
Part of Hodder and Stoughton
Carmelite House
50 Victoria Embankment
London EC4Y 0DZ

An Hachette UK Company

www.hachette.co.uk
www.hachettechildrens.co.uk

For Frank

Contents

Chapter One

Kit was packing his bag.

He was off to the palace to start a new job. He was going to be the Keeper of the King's Tights.

"Do a good job!" his mother
called after him.
"Be good to other people!"
called his father.

"Being the Keeper of the King's Tights is a very important job," explained the Keeper of the King's Cloaks. "The King is very attached to his tights."

Kit had never seen so many pairs
of tights. He only had one pair
himself but the King had hundreds.
There were tights of every colour.

There were thick tights and thin tights. Tights with swirling patterns. Tights with tinsel and glitter.

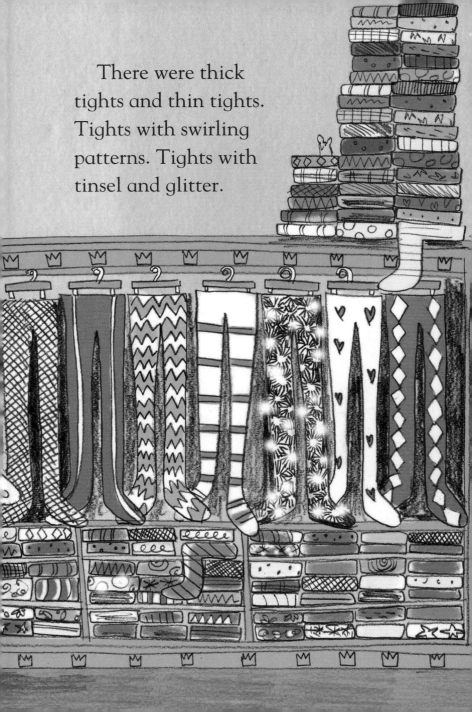

"Why does the King need so many tights?" Kit asked.

"He has a different pair for every occasion," said the Keeper of the King's Cloaks.

"Stretchy, stripy tights for riding . . .

strong, sturdy tights
for playing sports,

and shiny,
glittery tights
for parties."

17

"Which tights will the King want to wear today?" asked Kit. He was eager to start work.

"None of them," said the Keeper of the King's Cloaks. "The King is away. He is in the next kingdom, wooing."

"Wooing?" said Kit. He'd never heard of wooing before. He wondered what it was.

"Yes," said the Keeper of the King's Cloaks. "The King wants to marry the lovely Lady Linda. If the wooing goes well, there may be a wedding."

Chapter Two

Kit was sad not to see the King, but he kept himself busy with the tights.

He steamed them to make sure
they had no creases.

He puffed perfume at them so
they would smell sweet.

And he looked out for the tiny
moths that liked to munch holes.

Kit watched over the tights all
the time, night and day. He was
determined to do a good job.

Days went by, but the King did
not return.

"Will he be away much longer?"
Kit asked. "Will the wooing take a
long time?"

"That depends," said the Keeper
of the King's Cloaks. "It depends on
the lovely Lady Linda. She's lovely
but she's a tough nut to crack."

"I see," said Kit, although he
didn't really.

Soon Kit couldn't think of
anything else to do for the tights.
He had smoothed them and
stretched them until they looked
perfect.

"My legs could do with some
stretching too," Kit said to himself.
He walked round the rails of tights
a few times, but he needed a longer
walk than that.

"Maybe the tights will be all right on their own, just for a little while," Kit said.

He closed the windows, locked
the door and went for a stroll in the
palace grounds.

Chapter Three

While he was walking, Kit saw an old woman. She was leaning on a large sheep. Her eyes were closed and she was snoring.

"Hello," said Kit. "What are you doing? You look as if you should be in bed."

"I would be in bed if I could," said the old woman. "But the mice have eaten my mattress and I have nowhere to lay my head. I just catch five minutes now and again, wherever I can."

"That's terrible!" said Kit. "Poor you!"

Kit couldn't stop thinking about
the old woman who had nowhere
to lay her head. He ran back to the
Chamber of Tights and unlocked
the door.

He found a pair of the King's stripy riding tights and he took them down from their hanger.

Kit remembered the advice his mother and father had given him.

He really wanted to do a good job, but he wanted to be good to other people, too.

"The King has so many tights," Kit told himself. "I'm sure he won't miss these."

Kit used the tights to make a stretchy, stripy hammock. He strung it between two trees and he helped the old woman in.

She was very grateful.

"I'll sleep for a week now, thanks to you, Kit," she said.

Chapter Four

The next day, Kit's legs needed stretching again.

The tights were fine on their own yesterday, he thought, so they'll probably be fine today, too.

Kit found a trail of apples on the ground. He followed the trail until he met an apple-seller.

The apple-seller looked glum.

"Hello," said Kit. "What's the matter?"

"It's my cart," said the apple-seller. "It's got a huge hole in it and my apples keep falling out. I'll never get them to market now."

Kit thought for a moment and then he had an idea. The King wouldn't miss just one more pair of tights, would he?

Kit gave the apple-seller a pair of the King's strongest sports tights.

"Thanks, Kit," said the apple-seller. "This apple bag is brilliant!" He slung the bag over his shoulder and went on his way to market.

Kit enjoyed being good to other people. He liked helping them so much that he carried on doing it.

He helped a fisherman to mend his nets.

He helped a young cheese-maker
to strain her cheese.

And when the weather grew
colder, he helped a farmer to warm
up his cows.

Christmas came.

And then it was Spring, but there was still no sign of the King. Whatever wooing was, Kit thought, it was taking a very long time.

Chapter Five

One summer's day, Kit met a girl in a blueberry patch. She was jumping up and down like mad.

"Hello," said Kit. "Why are you doing all that jumping?"

"To scare away the birds, of course!" the girl said.

She pointed to a shabby old scarecrow. "That scarecrow's no use. If I stop jumping, the birds will eat all my blueberries."

"Maybe I can help," Kit said.

"I doubt it," puffed the girl.

Kit brought the girl a pair of the King's shiny, glittery tights – the ones he wore for parties. Kit cut the feet off the tights and put them in his pocket.

Then he dressed the old scarecrow
in the King's best party tights.
The tights twinkled in the
sunlight and scared the birds. They
flew away at once.
"Not bad, Kit," said the girl, and
she stopped jumping.

Just then there was a thundering
of hooves.

A group of fine horses galloped by.

"Who was that?" said Kit.

"Don't you know?" said the girl.
"It was His Majesty, the King!"

"The King?" said Kit.

"Of course it's the King," said the girl. "Who else would it be?"

But Kit was already running for the palace.

Chapter Six

Kit ran to the Chamber of Tights as fast as he could.

The Keeper of the King's Cloaks was already outside the door. And so was the King!

"Greetings, boy!" said the King.
"And good news! The lovely Lady
Linda is visiting, and I am throwing
a party in her honour! If it's a really
good party, she might even marry
me! I'll need a pair of my finest
party tights. At once, if you please!"

The King flung open the door.
Kit felt sick.

The Chamber of Tights was empty. Kit had given away all the King's tights. Every single pair!

"Where are all my tights?" said the King. "Whatever can I wear to the Lady Linda's party?"

Kit didn't know what to say. He felt sure he was about to lose his job, maybe even his head.

"You can wear these, Your Majesty," said a voice.

It was the girl from the blueberry patch. She appeared next to Kit and bowed to the King. She reached into Kit's pocket and pulled out what was left of the King's glittery party tights.

"What, in my kingdom, are those?" said the King.

"Party socks," the girl replied. "Sparkly, spangly ones. These socks are the latest fashion, Your Majesty."

"A new fashion?" the King said.
"Why didn't I know about this?"
He put the socks on and twirled in
front of the mirror.

Kit and the girl looked at one
another, and held their breath.

At that moment, the lovely Lady Linda put her head round the door.

"My word, Your Majesty!" she said to the King. "I never knew you had such handsome knees! Why didn't you tell me? I've always longed for a man with knees like that! Will you marry me?"

"Oh, hurrah!" said the King.
"I will! I'll marry you tomorrow!"
And he swept Lady Linda right off
her feet.

The next day, the King and the lovely Lady Linda were married.

Kit had a special seat right at the front. And he wasn't just Kit any longer.

He was *Sir* Kit now.

Sir Kit, the Keeper of the King's Socks.